KWAME LOVES THE AFRICAN DRUMS

Thank you

2024

KWAME LOVES THE AFRICAN DRUMS

Written &
Illustrated
by
Namibia EL

First Printing, December 2020

ISBN 979-8-5590-9592-9

Legacy Learning Books
P.O. Box 1777
Bellmawr, NJ 08099

www.leagacylearningbooks.com

DEDICATION

---To Robert and Wanda Dickerson, Founders and Directors of the Universal African Dance and Drum Ensemble (UAD),

I want to express my gratitude for everything you have helped me achieve here. You lead by example, educating people about the beauty of African culture and history through the arts. I appreciate you and thank you. Without you, this book would not have been possible.

"We must display and be the beauty, righteousness, and love of our original culture."--Robert Dickerson

The Universal African Dance and Drum Ensemble (UAD) has been prominently recognized and honored as one of the best professional, authentic African dance and drum ensembles in the United States of America by scholars, leaders, historians, and educators. The drums highlighted in this book are played by the musicians of UAD.

For more information about the Universal African Dance and Drum Ensemble please visit:

www.unitycommunity.com

Kwame loves the drums.
He loves each and every drum.

Each drum is profound.
Each drum has a special sound.

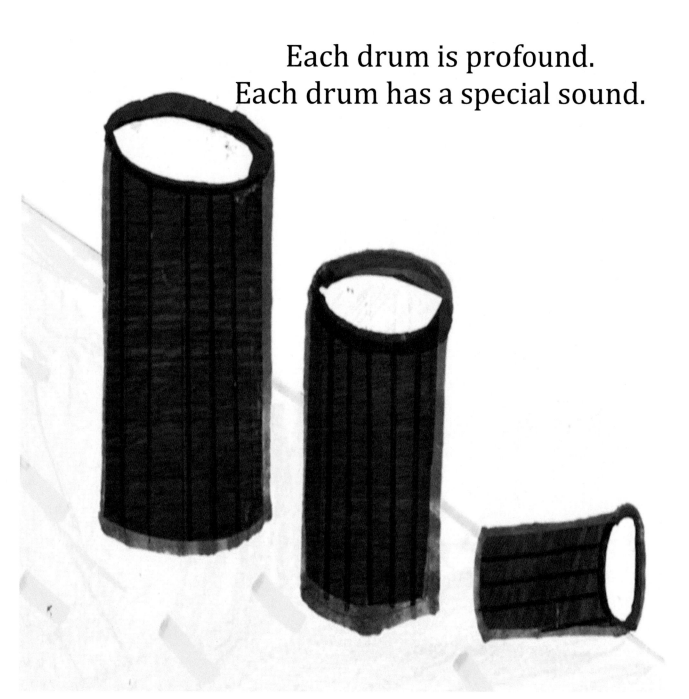

BOOM!
BOOM!
BOOM!

4

Kwame moves to the **djun djun** (JOON-joon).

BRUM!
BRUM!
BRUM!

He snaps his thumbs to the **tama** (TAA-muh) drum.

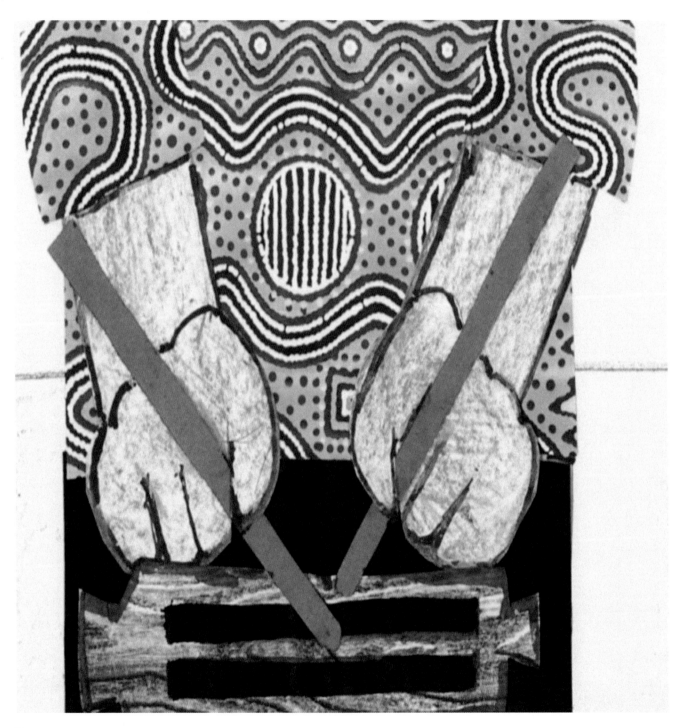

8

RIC-KA-TEE
RIC-KA-TEE
RIN!

The taps on the
krin (KREN)
makes him grin.

Oh, how Kwame loves
the African drums!

So many different shapes, sizes, and sounds.

BOP!
BOP!
BOP!

goes the **sangban**
(SUHNG-buhn).

PING!
PING!
PING!

goes the bell
on the **kenkeni**
(KIN-kuh-nee).

KABOOM!

KABOOM!

KABOOM!

goes the
doundoumba.
(DOON-doom-buh).

Kwame loves
the African
drums.
He loves
each and
every drum.
But most of all…

Kwame loves the **djembe** (JEM-bay) drum.

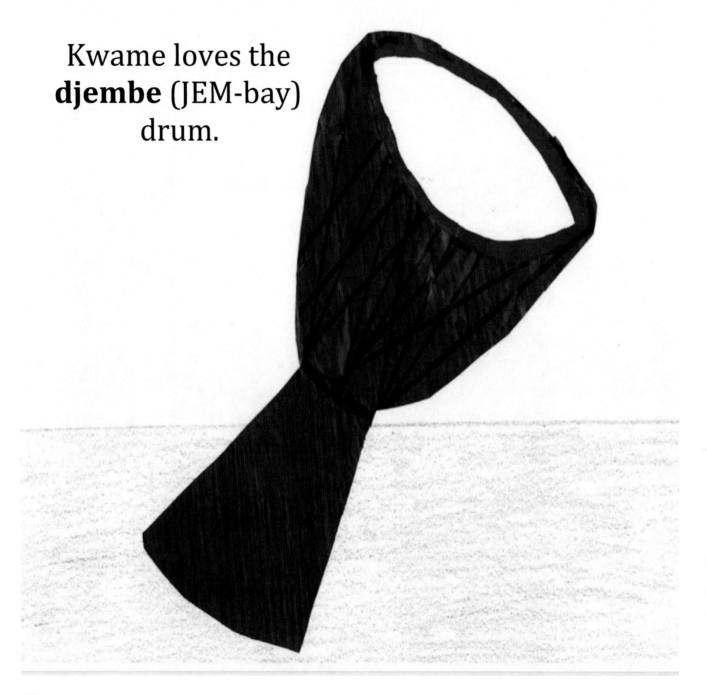

He loves to play
the djembe.

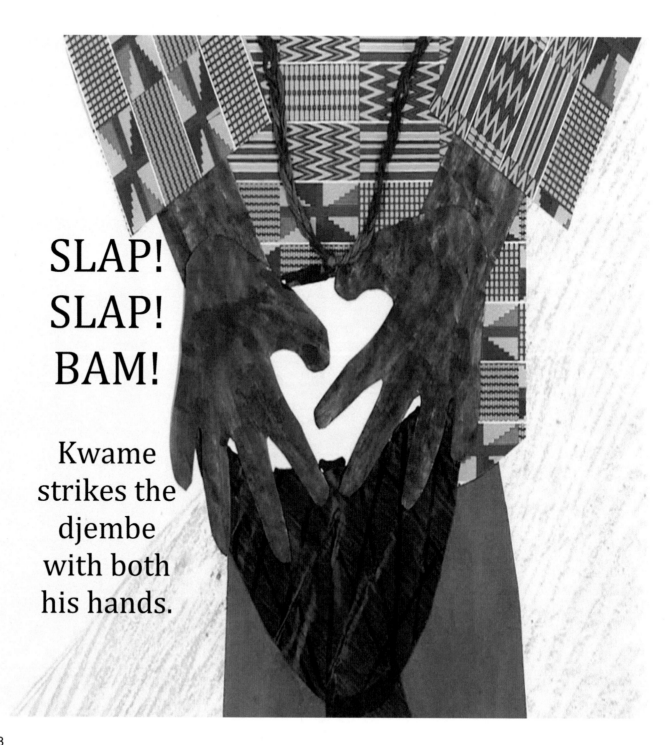

**SLAP!
SLAP!
BAM!**

Kwame
strikes the
djembe
with both
his hands.

He plays beats low.
He plays beats high.

He
plays
his
drum
in
the
djembe
line.

He plays beats fast.
He plays beats slow.

to signal the dancers to start the show!

There's so much to love about the African drums: the style, the tones, and the beats. Each drum looks and sounds unique.

Kwame loves the African drums.
He loves each and every drum.

But most of all...

Kwame loves the djembe.

ABOUT THE AFRICAN DRUM

Dance and drum started in the continent of Africa where all music begins. Traditionally, the African drum is used to gather people together, communicate, celebrate and for spiritual healing. There are a wide range of drums from many countries across the continent of Africa and the world. This book highlights the Djembe family of drums, which originated in West Africa. Making these drums require special skills and effort. First, African craftsmen cuts and hollows a tree trunk to create the drum's body or shell. Then, they expertly carve the drum to just the right shape. Finally, the craftsmen spread the skin of an animal over the head of the drum and used strong string, cord, or animal skin to tune the drum for different levels of sound. Each drum has its own unique sound, but when played together in an ensemble, it makes an electrifying harmony of music.

Djembe (JEM-bay)
The most popular of the African drums is the Djembe. It is the lead drum. The goblet-shaped body or shell is carved from hardwood. The head is made with goat skin and is played with the hands.

The Tama (TAA-muh) talking drum has an hourglass shaped body with two drumheads. It is played with a curved stick while squeezing the cords between the arm and body. Most talking drums sound like a human humming depending on the way they are played.

The Krin (KREN) is a log drum from West Africa. It is made from a solid piece of hardwood and is hollow inside, with slit openings, and a handle on each end. It is played with two wooden sticks.

The Sangban (SUHN-buhn) or Sanbeni (SUHNG-buh-nee) is the middle sized Djun Djun drum. It produces powerful, mid-range bass tones. Headed with cowhide on top and bottom, the Sangban is played with wooden sticks. [Sangban drum shown in middle]

The Doundoumba (DOON-doom-bah) or Dununba (DOO-noon-bah) is the largest Djun Djun drum. It produces a powerful low bass tone. Like the other Djun djun drums, this drum is headed with cowhide (on top and bottom) and is played with two wooden sticks. [Doundoumba drum shown on left]

The Djun Djun (JOON-joon) or Dunun (DO-noon) is the generic name for the family of West African drums that have developed together with the djembe. It is a rope-tuned cylindrical drum with cow skin at both ends, and played with one or two wooden sticks.

The Kenkeni (KIN-kuh-nee) drum, with the bell, is also known as a lead drum. It is the smallest of the Djun Djun drums. It has cow skin on both ends. The payer can produce two different sounds by striking the head with a wooden stick and tapping the bell with a piece of metal at the same time. [Kenkeni drum shown on top]

Made in the USA
Middletown, DE
08 June 2023

32264396R00020